To Mum and Dad,
who stopped smoking
~ J.C.

To Ruth with love
~ B.C.

Text copyright © 2002 by Jane Clarke.
Illustrations copyright © 2002 by Ben Cort.

Published by Troll Communications L.L.C.

Published by arrangement with Little Tiger Press, London.

ISBN 0-8167-7457-9

Printed in the United States of America.

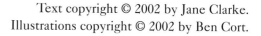

10 9 8 7 6 5 4 3 2

Smoky
Dragons

Jane Clarke   Ben Cort

Troll

The dragons' cave was full of smoke. Dad was smoking, and his daughter, Ember, flapped her wings in frustration.

"Dad," Ember said, "have you ever tried to stop?"

"Of course not, dear," her father replied with a cough. "Every grown-up dragon smokes."

"Well, I think you should quit. Your teeth are all yellow, you've got bad breath, and our cave stinks of smoke."

"That's exactly the way I like it,"
said Dad. "Dragons *always* smoke."

Ember's little brother, Burnie, was playing with his set of model knights. He loved the way the smoke came out of his dad's nostrils.

"Look, Dad, Burnie thinks it's cool to smoke!" said Ember.

"So he should! When he grows up, he'll want to be like his dear old dad."

"You wheeze when you fly," Ember pointed out. "You cough all the time. Smoking is bad for you!"

"I've told you," Dad answered patiently. "Dragons *always* smoke."

"Ember's right, Puffy dear," said Mom.

She had been sitting on the nest for the last two hundred years. It was easy to forget she was there.

"Our egg will be hatching soon," Mom continued. "*Egg Care* magazine says smoking is bad for young dragons. We must both try to stop."

"Stop smoking? You want me, Smoulder P. Smoke, to stop smoking?" asked Dad.

"Yes, Puffy dear," Mom replied, fluttering her big emerald eyes. "For the sake of our children, I do."

"Well, Char my love, if you say so, then I shall try to stop. But it won't be easy. Dragons *always* smoke."

At breakfast time, Ember floated into the kitchen. "Hey, the smoke is clearing already. Dad, you're *huge!* I've never seen all of you before."

"I don't know why you're so cheerful," Dad growled. "Who's eaten all the Knight Krispies?"

"You're very grumpy," said Ember.

"It's hard to stop smoking," Mom explained with a sigh.

"It will get easier," Ember told her.

"I doubt it," Dad grumbled. "Dragons *always* smoke."

The next day, Dad was hiding in the forest. Clouds of smoke were billowing out between the trees, and he didn't notice Ember sneaking up on him.

"Dad!" Ember cried. "You're smoking again! Mom will be mad at you."

"Who, me?" said Dad, trying to flap away the smoke. "I'm sure your mother will understand. Dragons *always* smoke."

"We need something to take our minds off it," said Mom. "Something nice to chew. Why don't you fly to the castle and see if they've got any fresh knights?"

"Fresh knights!" squeaked Burnie. "Yummy!"

Dad spread his wings. Ember and Burnie found it hard to keep up.

"Wow, Dad!" Ember exclaimed. "You're not wheezing! You can fly really fast when you don't smoke."

"We're in luck," said Dad. "There's been another delivery."

The fresh knights had just arrived at the castle. They hadn't seen a dragon before, so they were very easy to catch.

"Mmmm," said Mom, rubbing her tummy. "Fresh knights are scrumptious. I couldn't taste them properly when I was smoking."

"Delicious," agreed Dad. "Crunchy on the outside and soft and chewy in the middle."

"Oh, Puffy, you've still got the wrappers on!"

"What's that noise?" asked Ember.

"It's Dad eating," said Burnie.

"No. Not the munching, chomping, gulping noise. The clanging, clattering, trumpeting noise outside. What's going on?"

Ember stuck her head
out of the cave. "An army of
knights is coming our way!" she yelled.

"Oh, goody, seconds!" said Burnie, licking his lips.
"How many?"

"Hundreds!" Ember warned him. "They look really mean."

"Quick, let's hide!" cried Mom.

The dragons ran all around the cave, flapping their wings wildly.

"I expect they're a teensy bit angry about us eating them," Dad said. "They've come to get us!"

"Ssshhh!" whispered Ember.
"They're coming closer."

"We're all going to die!" wailed Burnie, trembling from head to tail.

"There'll be no dragons left in the world! Dragons will become extinct!" sobbed Mom.

The dragons held their breath. The knights had stopped outside their cave!

"Can't see any smoke," said the first knight.

"Can't *smell* any smoke," said the second knight.

"Can't hear any coughing," said the third knight.

"There are no dragons living here!" they all said together. "Dragons *always* smoke!"

Then the army of knights turned and marched back over the hill.

"Phew!" Dad breathed a sigh of relief. "That was close. It's a good thing we stopped smoking."

Ember had to agree!